W9-CGP-308

Children's Stories

pi kids ®
publications international, ltd.

Cover and title page illustrated by Margie Moore

Copyright © 2007 Publications International, Ltd.
All rights reserved.

This publication may not be reproduced in whole or in part by any means whatsoever without written permission from

Louis Weber, C.E.O., Publications International, Ltd.
7373 North Cicero Avenue, Lincolnwood, Illinois 60712

Ground Floor, 59 Gloucester Place, London W1U 8JJ

Customer Service: 1-800-595-8484 or customer_service@pilbooks.com

www.pilbooks.com

Permission is never granted for commercial purposes.

p i kids is a registered trademark of Publications International, Ltd.

8 7 6 5 4 3 2 1

ISBN-13: 978-1-4127-8306-4
ISBN-10: 1-4127-8306-2

Contents

Contents

The Ant and the Grasshopper

A Tale of Hard Work

The Ant and the Grasshopper

Adapted by Catherine McCafferty
Illustrated by Jason Wolff

Summer had just begun. Animals and insects scurried about, enjoying the summer sun. "Summer's here! The best time of the year!" the Grasshopper sang.

A line of ants marched past, carrying bits of food. As they walked along, some crumbs fell. Before the ants could pick up the crumbs, the Grasshopper had eaten them.

The ant at the end of the line walked up to the Grasshopper.

"We've worked hard to gather this food," said the Ant. "You should have helped us."

"That's what's wrong with your summer song," the Grasshopper sang. "Summertime is for play, not work."

"Summertime is for getting all the food we will need for the winter," said the Ant.

"Winter is far away, I'd rather go and play," said the Grasshopper, turning away.

"Wait!" cried the Ant. "What about the food you took from us?"

The Grasshopper pointed toward a field. "There's a whole field of wheat to replace your crumbs," he called, heading off to a nearby cornfield.

The Grasshopper quickly forgot about the Ant and leaped onto a cornstalk, where a soft leaf gave him a bed, and another, shade.

"Those ants can work and store. I choose to snooze and snore." He fell fast asleep.

Meanwhile, the Ant lined the tunnels of his home with food and seeds. "When the snow is on the ground, we will be full and warm in our nest," thought the Ant.

All that summer, the Grasshopper trailed the ants, eating his fill of the food they found and resting while they worked to store it.

Then one day, the Grasshopper heard a loud noise. The farmer was harvesting the corn! "I just lost my bed and food!" he cried.

A line of ants was marching past and heard the Grasshopper. The Ant stopped. "The days are getting shorter, my friend," he said. "But there is still time for you to store food and find a winter shelter."

"Not today, I've got to play," sang the Grasshopper, hopping through the grass.

He came across a promising spot under the shade of an old oak tree. But as soon as he had gotten comfortable, he heard a plop!

"Oh, I'm sorry," exclaimed a squirrel in the tree above him. "I'm collecting acorns for the winter. The more the better!"

As the Grasshopper soon saw, the field was filled with squirrels gathering nuts.

The squirrels chattered to one another, "Have you heard? This winter is going to be very snowy!"

All this work was making it very hard to play, and to sleep. The Grasshopper hopped through the field and came across a warm, sunny rock. He was just settling down when the ants began marching by.

"You again!" he said to the Ant. "I was sure that by now you'd have enough. You can't eat all that stuff!"

"It's always better to have a little extra than not enough," the Ant called.

The Grasshopper frowned. The sun had moved, and the rock was now cold.

The Grasshopper hopped off to the apple orchard and found a few small apples on the ground. He munched on them until he was full. Then he settled in for a nap near the root of the tree. The Grasshopper shivered. The sun had already set. "Someone needs to tell the sun that its working day is not done," he sang unhappily.

The sun was one thing the Grasshopper didn't mind seeing at work. With each day, though, it seemed to work less and less.

The ground seemed colder, too. One day, when the Grasshopper tried to nibble an apple, he found that it was frozen. "I don't like my apple in ice," said the Grasshopper.

He was so chilly that it was hard for him to think of a second line to his rhyme. "Ice, nice, rice, mice. . . ."

Then he thought, "Maybe I'll visit my friends, the mice." The Grasshopper crept into the home of the field mouse family, where it was so nice and warm inside.

"Thank you for visiting," said Mother Mouse. "I would invite you to stay, but all of my sisters and brothers are moving in for the winter. Isn't that wonderful? Oh, here they are now!"

A crowd of mice rushed into the nest. The Grasshopper was out of luck at the Mouse house.

The Grasshopper hopped back to the orchard. The ground was so cold that it hurt his tiny feet. "Where are those ants, now that I need them?" sang the Grasshopper.

Suddenly snow began to fall. He had to get inside or he would freeze! Hopping as fast as he could, the Grasshopper raced to the Ant's home. "Is anybody home?" he called.

"Why aren't you out playing in the snow?" asked the wise Ant.

The Grasshopper wanted to say he was just visiting. But he could feel the cold wind on his back. Sadly, the Grasshopper sang, "I should have listened to what you said. Now I'm cold and scared and unfed."

It wasn't his best song, but he hoped the Ant would understand.

He did. But he wanted to be sure that the Grasshopper understood, too. "We got our food for the winter by working hard. If you stay with us, you'll have to work hard, too."

The Grasshopper gulped. But then he remembered the ice and snow.

"Your job will be to sing for us," laughed the Ant. "Because winter is our time to play!"

All that winter, the Grasshopper sang for the Ant and his family. And the next summer, the Grasshopper sang a song as he helped to gather food. "Summer work is slow and steady. When winter comes, I will be ready!"

· Hard Work ·

The ants in this story worked very hard all summer, gathering food for the long winter ahead. They took pleasure in doing their job well. Because they planned ahead, they were able to play and enjoy the winter.

On the other hand, the Grasshopper chose to play all summer, and he had no food or shelter when the weather got colder. The Grasshopper thought the ants' work was no fun, but he soon learned that it was no fun to be cold and hungry, either.

The ants taught the Grasshopper that there is a time for work and a time for play, and each makes the other possible.

The Twelve Dancing Princesses

A Tale of Kindness

The Twelve Dancing Princesses

Adapted by Sarah Toast
Illustrated by Pamela R. Levy

Long ago there lived a king who had twelve beautiful and clever daughters. He loved his daughters, but he was becoming concerned about what they did each night. Even though the king carefully locked the door of the princesses' room every night, the next morning he found the princesses tired and out of sorts. More puzzling still, their dancing slippers were worn to shreds. Every day, the king had to order twelve new pairs.

The next morning, when the king begged his daughters to explain, the princesses merely murmured, "Papa, we have been sleeping peacefully in our beds all night."

The king wanted to know the truth, so he issued a proclamation declaring that the first man to find out where the princesses went to dance every night would choose a wife from among them. However, each had only three days and three nights to succeed.

A young prince soon arrived at the palace, and was given a small chamber next to the princesses' room. The door between the rooms was left open, so the princesses could not leave without the prince seeing.

That night, the prince gladly accepted a cup of wine offered to him by the eldest princess. In no time, he was sound asleep.

The next morning, when he awoke, the princesses were still asleep, with twelve pairs of worn-out shoes at the feet of their beds.

The next two nights, the same thing happened. As prince after prince met the same fate, the king began to despair of ever discovering his daughters' secret.

Then one day a poor soldier arrived in the kingdom. He had no sooner sat down by the side of the road to eat some bread and cheese when an old woman appeared all dressed in rags.

"Won't you share my meal?" offered the kind soldier, handing the woman his food.

"I am on my way to the castle," he continued. "I am going to try to find out how the princesses wear out their shoes."

The old woman surprised the soldier by saying, "Do not drink the wine the princess offers you. Pretend to fall asleep. Take this cloak, which will make you invisible. Follow the princesses and discover their secret!"

The soldier thanked the old woman and hurried on his way.

In the evening, the soldier was led to the chamber next to the princesses' room. The eldest princess offered him a cup of wine.

The soldier pretended to drink the wine, then pretended to fall asleep.

When the princesses were satisfied that the snoring soldier was asleep, they put on their dancing shoes. Then the eldest princess tapped on her bedpost three times. The bed sank into the floor and revealed a long, winding staircase.

One by one, the princesses stepped down into the opening. The soldier threw on the magical cloak and followed them.

But on the stairs, the soldier stumbled in his excitement and stepped on the bottom of the youngest princess's gown. She shrieked with alarm.

At last they came to a marvelous forest with trees of silver, gold, and diamonds. As they passed each type of tree, the soldier broke off a branch. Each time, the youngest princess cried out. Each time, the eldest princess told her there was nothing to fear.

The twelve princesses hurried to the edge of a lake, where twelve princes awaited them in twelve boats.

The soldier quickly hopped into a boat with the youngest princess and her prince, who observed, "Doesn't our boat seem a bit heavy tonight?"

On the other side of the lake stood a magnificent castle.

As they approached the shore, a fanfare of trumpets announced their arrival, and fireworks lit up the sky.

The princes and the princesses stepped into the great castle, where beautiful, lively music welcomed them into the ballroom. The laughing princesses danced with their princes for half the night.

Soon the princesses' slippers were worn out. The princes rowed the princesses back across the lake, and this time, the soldier rode with the eldest sister. The princesses bade their princes good night, and promised to return the next night. Then the princesses hurried back the way they had come.

The princesses were so tired that they slowed down at the top of the last set of stairs. The soldier was able to dash ahead of them, throw off his cloak, and jump into bed.

The princesses dragged themselves into their room and put their tattered shoes in a row. The eldest princess checked on the soldier and said to her sisters, "We are safe!" With that, all twelve sisters fell fast asleep.

The soldier followed the princesses the next night and the next. On the third night, he took a golden cup from the ballroom.

The next morning the king asked him, "Good soldier, have you discovered where my daughters dance their shoes to shreds?"

"Your Highness, I have," said the soldier. "They sneak down a hidden staircase. Then they walk through an enchanted forest to a beautiful lake. Twelve princes row them to a castle where they dance the night away."

Then the soldier showed the king the golden cup and the branches of silver, gold, and diamonds. The king called his daughters, who admitted the truth.

The king told the soldier to choose his wife. The soldier had already decided that he liked the eldest princess best. For her part, she thought the soldier was clever and kind.

They married at once, and the wedding guests happily danced the night away.

• Kindness •

The poor soldier was kind to the old woman, who was a stranger to him. In return, she helped him solve the mystery of the twelve dancing princesses. The soldier didn't have much food, but he shared because it was the right thing to do. He did not think the old woman was wealthy, and he did not expect a reward for his kindness. He knew that kindness is its own reward.

Have you ever done something nice for someone? Did it make you feel good to make someone else happy? Did you expect a reward for your good deed?

The Brave Little Tailor

A Tale of Ingenuity

The Brave Little Tailor

Adapted by Jennifer Boudart
Illustrated by Jeremy Tugeau

One morning, a little tailor sat in his shop. Suddenly the tailor had a taste for raspberry jelly. He took out a loaf of bread and cut a big slice from it, licking his lips as he spread on some jelly.

The tailor wanted to sew a little bit more before his snack. When he looked up again, a swarm of flies was buzzing around his jelly.

The little man waved the flies away with his hand. But they flew right back.

The tailor grabbed a scrap of cloth and growled, "Now I'll let you have it!" The cloth whooshed as he beat at the buzzing flies.

When he had finished, seven flies lay dead on the table. "The whole world should know of my skill!" said the tailor. He cut a belt just his size. With his finest thread, he sewed the words "Seven in one blow!"

He tied the belt around his waist and shouted, "I feel the need for an adventure!"

The tailor looked for something useful to take with him, but all he found was an old piece of cheese. He put it in his pocket. As he locked the door, he heard a rustle in the bush. A bird was trapped among the thorns.

The tailor gently pulled the bird from the brush. He put it in his pocket with the cheese. Then he set off to find his adventure.

The tailor walked through town and up a mountain. At the top, he met a giant. "Hello, Giant," said the tailor with a bow. "I am on a big adventure. Will you join me?"

"Me, join a little man like you?" rumbled the giant. For an answer, the tailor showed the giant his belt. The giant read the words stitched there: "Seven in one blow!"

The giant, who wasn't too smart, thought that the belt meant seven men, not flies. He found it very hard to believe that this tiny tailor could kill seven men with one blow.

7 in one

The giant decided to test the little man's strength. "You must be very strong," he said. "Can you do this?" He picked up a stone and squeezed until water dripped from his hand.

The tailor was not as strong as the giant, but he was much more clever. He pulled the cheese from his pocket and squeezed until liquid ran from his palm.

"Well, can you do this?" the giant asked. He picked up another stone and tossed it high into the air. It flew almost out of sight.

"Watch this," the tailor said as he took something else from his pocket. It was the bird, of course, which the tailor sent flying. Pretty soon the bird was out of sight!

This didn't convince the giant. "If you're so strong, help me move this tree," he asked.

The tailor quickly came up with a plan. He walked to the leafy end and said, "I'll carry the heavy branches. It is no trouble for one who can kill seven in one blow."

The giant lifted the tree trunk onto his shoulder. The tailor hopped into the branches and let the giant do all the work. When the giant stopped to rest, the tailor jumped out and pretended to be carrying the leafy end.

"You must be exhausted!" the giant said, a gleam in his eye. He insisted on taking the tailor to his cave to rest. The other giants were sitting down to eat when they arrived.

After dinner, the giant said, "You can sleep here," and pointed to a giant-size bed.

The tailor was a bit suspicious, so he hid in a corner. He watched the giants pound the bed with heavy clubs. They believed they had finally taken care of the pesky tailor.

In the morning, the giants swam in the river. When the tailor appeared, they were so afraid, they ran away without their clothes! The tailor laughed and left the giants behind. Along the road he met some soldiers. One saw the tailor's belt and decided to bring him to meet their king. The king was pleased, and hired the tailor for his army. He also gave him a bag full of gold.

But the other soldiers were jealous. "We will leave your army if we don't get a bag full of gold, too," they told the king.

The king could not lose his army. He decided to get rid of the tailor. "Go kill two giants living in my woods. Your reward will be my daughter's hand and half my land."

The tailor knew this was his chance to become a hero. This was adventure, all right!

The next morning, the tailor rode off to find the giants. "Stay behind until I call you," he told the soldiers who had come with him.

The tailor found the two giants asleep under a tree. He climbed the tree and began dropping acorns on one giant's head.

The giant awoke and turned to the other. "Why did you wake me by thumping my head?" roared the first giant.

Before the second could answer, the angry first giant threw an acorn at him. The two giants fought each other until both fell. The tailor called the king's soldiers to show them what he had done. They were amazed.

"Two giants are easy," said the tailor. "Try seven in one blow."

The king was impressed, but he had one more task. "Bring me a unicorn," he asked.

The tailor soon found one. In fact, it was running straight for him! At the very last second, the tailor jumped out of the way.

He had been standing in front of a tree, and the unicorn's horn stuck into the wood. The tailor freed it and rode the unicorn back.

The king had no choice but to keep his promise. He could not prove that the man who married his daughter and took half his kingdom wasn't anything but a hero.

The tailor almost gave up his secret one night, though. In his sleep, he said, "This new fabric will make a fine waistcoat."

His wife leaped from the bed, listening closely. But, awakened by the movement, he cleverly continued, "A man who can kill seven with one blow should have the finest waistcoat around. Right?"

· Ingenuity ·

The tailor was not big and strong, but he was very clever. He used his wits to outsmart giants, the king and his soldiers, and even a unicorn! Rewarded for his smarts with half of a kingdom and the hand of a princess, the tailor proved that you don't have to be a giant to be a giant-size hero.

A small person will often surprise you with a big heart or big ideas. Have you ever thought you knew what a person was like, and then he or she did something you never expected? Have you ever used your own ingenuity when up against a bully? What did you do?

The City Mouse and the Country Mouse

A Tale of Appreciation

The City Mouse and the Country Mouse

Adapted by Lisa Harkrader
Illustrated by Dominic Catalano

Once upon a time a country mouse named Oliver lived in a hole under the root of a big, old oak tree. He loved the smell of rich dirt and hearty grass all around him.

One fine fall day Oliver decided to invite his city cousin, Alistair, for a visit.

When Alistair arrived, he set his leather suitcase down and remarked, "I say, cousin, is this your cellar?"

"No," replied Oliver, "it's my home."

Oliver showed Alistair the back of the hole, where he stored his grain. He led his cousin up onto the knob of the old oak root, where he sometimes sat to watch the sunset. Then he sat Alistair down at the tuna-can table and served him a dinner of barleycorn and wheat germ.

Alistair nibbled his meal politely. "This certainly tastes as though it's good for me." He coughed and swallowed. "A bit dry, though, perhaps. Could I bother you for a cup of tea?"

Oliver brewed up a thimble of dandelion tea for them both. "Here's to my cousin Alistair! Thanks for visiting," toasted Oliver.

Oliver awoke early the next morning, as usual. A robin family twittered in the old oak tree. A rooster crowed at a nearby farm.

Alistair squeezed his pillow over his ear. "Oh, dear. What is that confounded racket?" he mumbled.

"That's the sound of morning in the country," said Oliver cheerfully.

Alistair pulled the pillow from his face and opened one eye. "You start your day in the morning?" he asked.

"Here in the country we rise at dawn," Oliver said. "We'd better start the chores."

Alistair reluctantly pulled on a pair of overalls and followed his cousin outside.

CITY

While Oliver set to work, Alistair leaned against the root of the old oak tree. After some time, Oliver returned with corn, rye, and acorns, which he piled neatly.

"Thank goodness you're done," Alistair said, collapsing into a wheelbarrow.

Oliver giggled. "We still have lots to do."

Alistair sighed. "I'm simply not cut out for the country life," he said. "A mouse could starve to death here. Come home with me for a while. I'll show you the good life."

Alistair packed his silk pajamas into his fine leather suitcase. Oliver packed his long johns into his beat-up carpetbag. The two mice set out for Alistair's home in the city.

Oliver followed Alistair over fields and valleys, into dark, noisy subway tunnels, and through crowded city streets, until they reached the luxury hotel where Alistair lived.

Oliver stared up at the revolving glass door in front of him. "H-h-how do we get inside, Alistair?"

"Wait till the opening comes around, then run through," Alistair replied. The door swung around, and Alistair swiftly disappeared inside. It took a few more spins before Oliver gave it a try.

Oliver followed Alistair across the beautifully decorated lobby and through a small crack in the wall.

Hotel
DeLuxury

DeLuxury

"My apartment," Alistair said when they were inside.

Oliver looked around in amazement. His cousin's home was filled with crystal goblets and linen napkins. The little apartment was lovely, but so different from Oliver's home in the old oak tree.

"We're under the bandstand," Alistair pointed out. "An orchestra plays, and people dance every night until dawn."

"How can you sleep with all the noise?" asked Oliver.

"I sleep during the day," said Alistair. "We do some things a little differently here. Dinner, for example. Follow me!"

Alistair led Oliver through the dining room. They hid behind potted plants and raced under tablecloths. They waited until the chef went to check something in the dining room, then scampered across the kitchen and into the dark pantry.

They climbed up the shelves to the hors d'oeuvres. Alistair gobbled fancy crackers, nibbled pasta, and even managed to chew a hole in a tin of smoked salmon.

"Now this," said Alistair, patting his tummy, "is fine dining."

But all of the hiding and scurrying had scared Oliver. He barely ate a crumb. Alistair was too excited for the next course to notice.

"Tonight the chef is preparing roast duck with herbed potatoes," Alistair said, his mouth watering with anticipation.

Alistair began gathering up bits of food. He didn't notice the chef marching back into the kitchen.

But the chef noticed Alistair. "You again!" he shouted, chasing the mice with a broom.

Alistair and Oliver escaped through a hole under the sink.

"Don't worry," said Alistair. "We'll make up for the measly dinner with dessert."

Alistair showed Oliver the dessert cart. Oliver timidly nibbled the edge of a flaky cream puff. He leaned forward, and *splat!*

A waiter had bumped the cart, and now Oliver was facedown in the cream puff.

Oliver wobbled off the cart. "I'm not cut out for life in the city," he said. "You take too many risks for your dinner. A mouse could starve to death here, too. I'm going home to the good life."

So Oliver dragged his carpetbag back through crowded city streets, over fields and valleys until he reached his hole under the root of the big, old oak tree.

Back at his hotel, Alistair curled up in his bed and listened to the orchestra play.

Both mice sighed. "I love being home," they said.

• Appreciation •

There is no place like home! That's what the mice in this story believed, anyway. Though each mouse was willing to give the other's way of life a try, Alistair and Oliver both realized how much they appreciated their own homes. The bustling city life suited Alistair, while the quiet of the country was more Oliver's pace.

Have you ever stayed at a friend's house and noticed that things seemed strange or different from your house? That doesn't mean that your friend's house isn't good. You are probably more comfortable in your own home, with your own toys. This means you appreciate what you have.

Saint George and the Dragon

A Tale of Courage

Saint George and the Dragon

Adapted by Brian Conway
Illustrated by Tammie Speer Lyon

This is the tale of Saint George, an orphan boy who had been raised by fairies. Under their guidance, he grew up brave, calm, strong, courteous, quick, and clever. They taught him to be a noble knight.

At last the time came when George was old enough to seek his destiny. The queen of the fairies called him to see her.

"Your journey starts today," she told him. "You have many adventures before you."

"Yes, Your Majesty," George bowed.

"Always remember one thing," added the queen, tapping George's silver battle helmet. "Your greatest weapon is your mind."

With those words, George set off. He traveled through many wonderful kingdoms. But as George approached the town of Silene, he noticed the land change from lush and green to dark and desolate. There was no grass, only thick mud. It seemed the ground had been crossed by fire. The trees were bare and black, and a foul stench filled the air.

As George walked through this stark land, he did not see a soul—not a bird, not a squirrel, and certainly not a single person.

Soon George saw a castle enclosed by a high wall. When he got closer, George saw a young lady creep quietly through the gate.

"Excuse me," he called politely after her.

"Quiet!" she hushed him. "Leave now if you value your life."

"But I am a brave knight here to help you," George whispered.

"Alas, sir," the woman replied, "you are but one man. I fear that you cannot help."

George looked her in the eyes. "It is my destiny," he said. "I will not go until I have done all I can, even if it costs me my life."

"I am Princess Sabra," she finally said. "Come with me."

Sabra then explained why the kingdom lived in such fear.

A ferocious dragon had ravaged the land. Many men had tried to slay the dragon, but without success. The whole kingdom had moved inside the castle walls for protection.

But soon the dragon ran out of food.

"If you do not feed me sheep each day," the dragon had roared, "I will come through those walls for my breakfast!" So every day, the people provided food for the dragon.

"We gave up our last two sheep this very morning," said Sabra sadly. "Tomorrow we shall have nothing to give the dragon, and we shall all perish."

"Then I have arrived at just the right time," said George bravely.

They soon came to a cave. "To slay the dragon," Sabra told George, "we need help."

In this cave there lived a wise old hermit. When they arrived, he did not turn to look, but spoke as if he knew they were coming.

Long ago, it was told,
Two brave knights would come to know,
The only way to save the rest:
The Serpent's weakness is in his breath.

With that, an ancient hourglass appeared at their feet. George did not understand. He asked the strange little man, but the hermit would speak no more.

When George and Sabra left the cave, it was already dark. They hurried to the sleeping dragon's lair.

As they traveled, George remembered what the queen had said. His best weapon, she had told him, was his mind. He studied the hourglass closely. Each bit of sand looked like a magic crystal frozen in time.

They arrived at the lake. George and Sabra walked softly through the fog so they would not be heard. The sands in the hourglass dropped with every careful step.

"The hourglass will lead us," George whispered. "We must wait until all the sand has dropped through."

The smell as they approached the lair was horrible. George and Sabra watched the icy blue sands drop as the dragon snored.

Suddenly, the dragon stirred. With the sands still making their way through the hourglass, he raised up and rubbed his slimy eyes.

Just as the very last grain of sand was dropping through the hourglass, the dragon yawned a great, fiery yawn.

"Now, George!" Sabra shouted.

George knew what to do. He threw the magic hourglass up into the dragon's yawning mouth. It shattered on the dragon's slithering tongue in a cloud of icy mist.

The dragon reared back to hurl a fiery blast at George and Sabra. But, as fortune would have it, only cool ice and soft snow came from the dragon's mouth.

The hermit's magic had transformed the dragon! His mouth shut tight with ice, the once-fearsome dragon jumped into the deep, warm lake. Only there could he keep from freezing from the inside out.

That dragon never bothered another soul. Some say they have seen him coming up for air on occasion, but only on very warm nights. The dragon would not dare stay out of the warm water too long, for fear of becoming a giant icy statue.

George and Sabra had saved the kingdom. The two arrived at the castle to great cries of joy and triumph. The grateful people of Silene were no longer prisoners in their own kingdom.

The king offered George all he had in thanks, but George wanted no payment.

"I have many adventures left," George told the people. "They are my reward."

George continued on his journeys, sharing his tale along the way. People everywhere learned of his courage and selflessness. That is how George, the brave knight from the land of the fairies, earned his sainthood.

· Courage ·

When George agreed to fight the dragon that was wreaking havoc on the kingdom of Silene, he did not think of the danger that might come to him. He thought only of helping other people and making their lives better. He was truly brave.

Being brave can be a very hard thing to do, but there are lots of ways to show courage. Meeting new people can be a scary thing, but a good opportunity to show how brave you can be. If you smile and say hello, the other person will be happy that you did. It takes a courageous person to smile first.

The Golden Goose

A Tale of Generosity

The Golden Goose

Adapted by Brian Conway
Illustrated by Karen Dugan

There once was a gentle boy called Samuel. He lived near the forest with his family, who often treated him poorly.

One day Samuel's eldest brother went to cut wood. Their mother packed sweet cake and cider for his trip. In the woods, Samuel's brother came upon a little gray man.

The man said, "Will you share your meal with a tired old man?"

But Samuel's selfish brother refused.

The brother began to chop a tree. After a few strong swings, his ax slipped and cut him. He hurried home to dress his wound.

Now the second brother was called to get the firewood. Their mother also gave him sweet cake and cider for his journey. Before long the second brother also met up with the old man in the woods.

The man bid him good day and said, "Would you share your meal with a tired old man? I am very hungry and thirsty."

This middle brother was as selfish as the first. "If I give you my food and drink, I won't have enough for myself," he said. "Now get out of my way!"

The second brother walked away and found a tree to chop. But the head of the ax broke off and fell firmly on the brother's foot, and he, too, could no longer work. Samuel's second brother hobbled home.

Samuel said, "I'll cut the wood, Father."

"You know nothing about it," his father replied harshly. "But if you are so willing to get hurt, then go."

Samuel's mother handed him some stale bread and a jug of warm water. In the forest, Samuel met the little gray man as well.

The old man kindly bid him good day and said, "Would you share with a tired old man? I am so very hungry and thirsty."

"I have only stale bread and warm water," Samuel said, "but if you don't mind that, we can eat together."

But when Samuel reached for their snack, he found sweet cake and cider.

"My, look at this," said Samuel.

When they finished their tasty meal, the old man told Samuel, "You shared with me. Now you will have good luck to go with your kind heart."

The man pointed at an old tree nearby. "Cut that tree and you'll find something special there in its roots." Then the man walked away without another word.

Samuel did as the old man said.

Samuel raised his ax and swiftly cut down the old tree. When the tree fell, Samuel found a goose sitting among the roots. Its feathers were made of gold!

Samuel had never seen such a splendid sight! He picked up the goose and hurried into town. He had to share this great goose with everyone he knew.

Samuel beamed proudly as he carried his golden goose through the town. He passed an inn, and the innkeeper's three curious daughters came out to see the beautiful bird. Each of the three daughters wanted to take one of the goose's golden feathers to keep for her own.

When Samuel stopped to show them the goose, the eldest sister tiptoed behind Samuel and tugged at the goose's wing. Her hand stuck there tightly. She waved to her sisters for their help.

The sisters thought that together they could free her. They joined hands to pull. Instead, they found they were all stuck to each other! The sisters scurried behind Samuel, who marched toward the next town with his goose.

Samuel hurried through a field on his way to the next town. The girls followed closely behind. In the field, he passed a minister and his wife.

The minister saw the odd procession and cried out at the sisters, "Have you no shame, girls? Why must you run after the boy?"

The minister tried to pull the youngest girl away. All too soon he felt that he himself was stuck, and he had to run as fast as his legs could carry him to keep up.

The minister's wife saw her husband running along with the three girls. She pulled on his sleeve. Then she was caught up in this silly parade, too.

They passed two farmers on a road. The minister's wife called for help, but as soon as they touched her, the farmers were pulled along, too!

Samuel hurried into the next town, with everyone behind him. There a king lived with his only daughter. The princess was so serious that it was believed she could not laugh. The king proclaimed that whoever made the princess laugh would marry her.

Samuel happened to pass this castle. At the sight of this bumbling parade, the princess burst into fits of laughter.

Samuel asked her to marry him. But the king did not want Samuel to marry his daughter, so he gave him a challenge.

"Bring me a man who can drink a whole cellarful of cider, and eat a mountain of bread," he said, certain Samuel would fail.

Samuel thought of the little man in the woods and rushed off.

"Oh, I'm so thirsty and so very hungry," said the man to Samuel.

Back at the castle, the little man happily drank all the cider and ate all the bread.

But the king had another demand. "Bring me a ship that sails on both land and sea."

Again, Samuel went to see the little man.

"I will share my magic," said the old man, "because you have been so kind to me."

Soon Samuel was back at the castle with a ship that sailed on land and sea. The king had no choice but to let Samuel marry the princess. The two were married that very day.

• Generosity •

Even though his parents did not give him the same kind of treatment they gave his brothers, Samuel was very generous. He shared what little he had with the old man because it was better than letting the old man go hungry. Because the boy was so generous, the man rewarded him with many kindnesses.

Being generous and doing kind things for people will not always be rewarded with favors or special gifts. But the feeling of making someone happy during a time of need is a reward in itself.

Demeter and Persephone

A Tale of Love

Demeter and Persephone

Adapted by Megan Musgrave
Illustrated by Michael Jaroszko

Hades, the king of the Underworld, sat on his lonely throne. The Underworld was cold and dark and dreary, and the sun never shone. No one came to visit because the gates were guarded by Cerberus, a huge three-headed dog who scared everyone away.

"I need a companion to bring joy to this place," said Hades. He decided to disguise himself and go up to the earth's surface to find a companion.

There lived Demeter, the goddess of the harvest. She had a beautiful daughter named Persephone, who had long, golden hair and rosy cheeks. Happiness followed her wherever she went. Demeter was always full of joy when Persephone was near.

And when she was happy, the whole world bloomed. The fields and orchards were always full of crops to be harvested.

Persephone loved to run through the fields and help Demeter gather food for the people of the earth.

When Hades visited the earth, he saw Persephone playing in an apple orchard. He had never seen anything so beautiful!

Hades stood at the edge of the orchard and watched Persephone play.

Finally, she saw Hades. In his tattered cloak, he looked like a hungry traveler. Persephone was always generous, so she picked several apples from the tree and climbed down to meet him. "Please," said Persephone, "take these apples."

Hades thanked her and returned to the Underworld. "I must bring her here!" he thought. "It could never be gloomy with such a kind and beautiful queen as this!"

The next morning, Persephone ran to her favorite orchard and began picking the ripest apples she could find.

Suddenly there was a great rumble, and the ground split open before her! Out charged two fierce, black horses pulling Hades and his dark chariot behind them.

Persephone tried to run, but Hades was too quick for her. He caught her and took her away to the Underworld. The ground closed back up behind them.

When Demeter came home from the fields, Persephone was nowhere to be seen. Demeter went to the orchard where Persephone had been picking apples, and found some apples spilled on the ground.

"Something terrible has happened!" she cried, and ran to search for her daughter.

After looking everywhere, Demeter visited Helios, the god of the sun. "Helios sees everything on the earth. He will help me find Persephone," she said.

"I have seen her," Helios said. He told Demeter that Hades had taken Persephone to the Underworld to be his queen.

Demeter became sad and lonely for her daughter. The earth became cold and snowy, and the crops in the field faded and died.

In the Underworld, Persephone was sad and lonely, too. The ground was too cold to plant seeds, and there was no sunshine to help them grow. Finally she asked Hades to let her return to the earth.

"But you are my queen!" exclaimed Hades. "I am sure you will be happy here if you only stay a while longer."

Persephone had become friends with Cerberus. Although he looked ferocious, he was lonely just like her. But even with her new friend, Persephone missed the sunny days and lush fields of the earth.

Demeter missed her daughter more and more. Finally she traveled to Mount Olympus, the home of the gods. She asked Zeus, the most powerful god, for his help.

"Hades has taken my daughter to the Underworld to be his queen! Please help me bring her back!" begged Demeter.

Zeus saw that the earth had become cold and barren. He knew he had to help Demeter make it fruitful again. "I will ask Hades to return Persephone," said Zeus sternly. "But only if she has not eaten any food in the Underworld. Anyone who eats the food of the dead belongs forever to Hades."

"Hades!" thundered Zeus when he reached the gates of the Underworld. He made his way inside easily, for even fierce Cerberus was afraid of the king of the gods.

Zeus found Hades sitting sadly on his dark throne, watching Persephone, whose golden hair had grown dull, and whose once rosy cheeks were now pale.

"Hades, I demand that you return Persephone to the earth," said Zeus.

"Very well," sighed Hades. "I thought her beauty would make my Underworld a happier place, but she is only sad and silent since she has come. You may take her back to the earth."

But Hades was very clever, and decided to trick Zeus. Taking Persephone aside, Hades told her she would need food for her journey. He offered her a pomegranate, from which Persephone ate just six delicious seeds before she returned to the earth. She did not know that Hades had tricked her into eating the food of the dead.

Zeus carried Persephone from the dark Underworld. Demeter was so happy to see her daughter that the earth bloomed again.

Suddenly, Hades appeared, and cried, "Persephone ate six seeds from a pomegranate before she came back to the earth. She must live in the Underworld forever!"

Zeus was angry about the trick. Finally he said, "For each seed, you will spend one month of the year in the Underworld. The other six months you will spend on the earth."

Each year when Persephone goes to the Underworld, winter comes to the earth. But when Persephone returns, the earth blooms in celebration.

Persephone was a kind and gentle person who tried to find good in everyone. When Hades took Persephone to the Underworld, Demeter's love was so strong that she searched everywhere and asked for the gods' help in getting her back. Demeter loved her daughter so much that it even affected the seasons on the earth, bringing cold, barren winter when they were apart.

When you love someone very much, you will do anything for that person. Do you feel that way about someone? How do you show your love?

George Washington and the Cherry Tree

A Tale of Honesty

George Washington and the Cherry Tree

Adapted by Catherine McCafferty
Illustrated by Jerry Harston

Many stories and books have been written about George Washington. After the American colonies won their freedom, he served as the first president.

The legend of George Washington's honesty is just as famous as stories of his leadership and bravery. Did young George Washington chop down a cherry tree? Maybe not. But this legend shows just how important it is for everyone to tell the truth.

It was a fine day for young George Washington. At six years old, he had just received his very own hatchet. It felt solid in his small hands. George swung the hatchet through the air just to see the sun shine on it.

"A hatchet is not a toy, George," his father warned. "Always be careful when you use it."

George nodded at his father's words. A hatchet was a serious thing, indeed. George promised he would always be very careful with it.

Once he was outside, though, George felt more excited than serious. His family's farm seemed full of things to cut.

First George tested his hatchet on a row of weeds at the edge of the cornfield. It sliced through their thin stems. George smiled. Then he took aim at the thicker stalks of the corn plants.

Whack! Three cornstalks fell with a rustle and a crunch. George stepped back, startled. His father was right. He would have to be careful. Then George saw that an ear of corn had fallen to the ground. George's hatchet sliced the corncob in half with no problem.

Not far from the cornfield, George's father tended to his fruit trees. He kept the trees' branches trimmed, and watched them for any sign of sickness.

Mr. Washington gave extra attention to his youngest tree. It was a cherry tree, and it had come from far away. The tree had been just a sapling when Mr. Washington planted it. Each year, Mr. Washington watched it grow stronger, and thought of the sweet, fresh cherries it would give. He smiled to himself as he gave the cherry tree a pat.

George ran up to Mr. Washington as he walked back to the house for supper. "This hatchet works well, Father," he said.

His father smiled. "Yes, I've seen you using it."

"Thank you again, Father, for such a wonderful gift," said George as he ran inside.

During dinner, George excitedly told his mother all about his afternoon of testing his new hatchet.

"I think it's time you put that hatchet to good use, George," she said. "Tomorrow, I would like you to chop kindling for the fire."

That night, George put his hatchet under his bed, climbed in, and closed his eyes. But George had a hard time falling asleep. He couldn't wait until morning. He saw himself chopping piles, and then mounds, and then mountains of kindling! When George finally fell asleep, he dreamed that he was a great woodcutter. With one sweep of his hatchet, he cut down whole forests.

The next morning, George hurried through his breakfast. "I'm ready to chop kindling now," he told his mother.

In the woodshed, George went to work. He chopped the long, thin branches into small sticks. George chopped the small sticks into smaller and smaller pieces until they could be chopped no more. He ran inside to tell his mother that he had finished his job.

"I'm finished, Mother. Is there any more kindling for me to chop?" George asked.

"No, George. You may play for a while," she said.

George didn't want to play. He wanted to chop more wood.

George decided to test his hatchet again. He went to an old, thick fence post. The hatchet's blade sunk deep into the wood. "That was too thick," George thought. Then he saw the trunk of the young cherry tree.

The thin tree trunk looked just right. George chopped at it. The blade dug into the tree trunk, but pulled free easily. Why, it would take just a few strokes of his hatchet to cut the tree down!

George chopped until the tree fell. He was proud, until he remembered how much his father liked the cherry tree. Then he remembered how his father had told him to be careful with the hatchet.

Mr. Washington saw the fallen tree on his way to the house. Then he realized there would be no cherries. After all his hard work and care, there would be no cherry tree. He walked sadly back to the house.

George saw his father walk past the woodshed. Slowly, he followed his father into the house. He held his hatchet tight.

His father turned as he heard George come in the door. He looked at George. He looked at George's hatchet and asked, "Do you know who cut down my cherry tree?"

George took a deep breath and said, "I cannot tell a lie, Father. I cut down your cherry tree."

George looked at his feet. He felt like crying. "I wasn't careful with the hatchet. I'm sorry, Father." Then he held his breath and waited to hear his punishment.

To George's surprise, his father did not seem angry. In fact, he looked rather calm.

"You have been honest, Son," said Mr. Washington. "That means more to me than any cherry tree ever could."

George's father was disappointed that there would be no cherries, but he was proud of his son for telling the truth. "You must always be honest," George's father said.

George never forgot those words. They were a lesson for life.

· Honesty ·

Young George Washington was proud to have gotten his own hatchet. But he did not use good judgment, and cut down his father's cherry tree. When he realized what he had done, George did not try to hide the mistake. He knew the right thing to do was to tell his father the truth, no matter what his punishment might be.

Sometimes telling the truth seems scary. Did you ever tell the truth, even though you knew you might be punished? Even if you are afraid of what might happen, being honest is always better.

Thumbelina

A Tale of Patience

Thumbelina

Adapted by Megan Musgrave
Illustrated by Jane Maday

There was once a woman who had a lovely little cottage and the most beautiful garden around. But she was sad that she had no one to share them with.

So she asked the old witch in her village for help. The witch handed her a bag of seeds and instructed her to tend to them closely.

The woman took the seeds home with her. The next day, she planted them in a sunny corner of her garden. It was the prettiest spot she could find. She watered and watched over the seeds every day.

Soon tiny green sprouts began to poke up out of the ground. Before long, they blossomed into a patch of wildflowers.

In the center of the patch grew a single, beautiful tulip. The flower was so lovely that the woman could not resist bending down to smell it. Suddenly the petals opened, and the woman was amazed to find a tiny girl sitting inside. She wore a tulip petal for a dress.

"You are the most beautiful child I've ever seen," exclaimed the woman. "Would you like to stay with me in my garden?"

"Oh, yes!" replied the tiny girl.

"You're hardly as big as my thumb," said the woman. "I will call you Thumbelina."

The woman made a tiny bed out of an acorn shell. Thumbelina slept soundly under her rose-petal blanket.

Thumbelina and her mother lived very happily in the garden the whole summer long. Thumbelina loved to play in the little pond in the middle of the garden.

Sometimes, Thumbelina sang as she rowed. She had the most beautiful, silvery voice that her mother always loved to hear.

One day, a frog was hopping by. He heard Thumbelina singing. When he saw the tiny girl rowing her maple-leaf boat he said, "What a lovely creature! I must take her away to my lily pad to be my wife."

The frog hid behind the reeds until Thumbelina's mother went inside. Then he jumped out and captured the girl. He carried her away to the river where he lived and placed her on a lily pad. "Rest here while I go make plans for our wedding," said the frog.

Thumbelina did not want to be the wife of a frog. She wanted to be back home with her mother. She became so sad that she began to cry. Her tiny tears fell into the river and made ripples in its glassy surface.

When the fish saw Thumbelina crying, they decided to help her. They nibbled through the stem of her lily pad until it broke free and floated down the river.

Finally the lily pad came to rest on a grassy bank.

Thumbelina climbed up the bank and found herself on the edge of a meadow. "I miss my home, but this will be fine until I can find my way back again," she said.

She wove herself a tiny hammock out of grass blades and hung it up beneath a large daisy, which sheltered her from the dew at night. During the day she wandered through the meadow. She became friends with the butterflies and ladybugs in the meadow, and at night she slept safely under her daisy roof.

One day, Thumbelina noticed that the days were getting chilly. Fall was coming.

The nights were becoming colder, too. "How will I keep warm until I can get home?" cried Thumbelina.

One day, she found a small burrow inside a tree. She poked her head inside to see if anyone lived there.

Inside the little burrow lived a friendly old field mouse. The burrow was snug and cozy. "Excuse me," said Thumbelina politely, "may I please come into your warm burrow for a moment?"

The kind field mouse invited Thumbelina to stay with her for the winter. Thumbelina sang songs and danced, while the field mouse cooked dinner or sewed by the fire.

Together the new friends also feasted on nuts, grains, and berries they had gathered for the cold winter months. The air was chilly, and the very last of the crisp, brown leaves had long since fallen from the old oak tree.

One day it began to snow. Thumbelina had never seen snow before, so she opened the door to peek outside. But as she looked outside, she saw something strange. Near the field mouse's front door was a young sparrow with a broken wing. He was shivering and he looked sad.

Thumbelina called the field mouse, and together they helped the poor sparrow into the burrow.

The three new friends passed the rest of the winter together. Thumbelina told them stories of her kind mother and the beautiful garden where she had been born.

One day, Thumbelina poked her head outside the burrow again. Tiny green shoots were beginning to appear all over the meadow. "Spring is here!" she exclaimed.

The sparrow decided it was time to leave the burrow. "Thumbelina," he said, "you saved my life. Now I would like to help you, too."

Thumbelina said good-bye to her field mouse friend and held on tight to the sparrow's back as he soared above the trees.

"I have something special to show you," said the sparrow. He flew deep into the forest and landed gently in a thicket. Suddenly, a lily opened and out stepped a tiny boy. He wore a crown on his head, and he had a pair of shiny wings.

"I am the Prince of the Flowers," he said. "Live with us and be our princess."

She agreed, but asked first to see her mother. When she and the prince flew to her mother's cottage, the woman was overjoyed to see her daughter. She invited the prince and all of the other fairies to come live in her beautiful garden, where the sparrow and field mouse came every year to visit.

• Patience •

Away from home, Thumbelina was alone and a little scared. But she never gave up hope of returning to her mother and the beautiful garden. Thumbelina was patient, and kind to every creature she met along her journey back home. Even though she was away from her mother, she enjoyed the company of her new friends, and did all she could to help them. Her patience was rewarded, and she was able to get home.

Did you ever want something very badly when you knew you had to wait for it? If you are patient, the waiting will not seem so bad.

A Brer Rabbit Story

A Tale of Ingenuity

A Brer Rabbit Story

Adapted Megan Musgrave
Illustrated by Rusty Fletcher

Brer Rabbit was the craftiest rabbit ever to cross a fox's path, and Brer Fox was always trying to catch him. One day, Brer Fox decided to get Brer Rabbit once and for all.

Brer Fox knew that Brer Rabbit liked to go over to the farmer's garden every day for carrots and cabbage. Brer Fox decided to hide behind a big tree and wait for Brer Rabbit to pass. The tree was on the edge of a briar patch, full of bushes with thorns and burrs.

Soon Brer Rabbit came hippity-hopping down the road. Brer Fox jumped out and grabbed him up as quick as he could.

"I'm a-gonna brew a stew out of you, Rabbit!" said Brer Fox.

Brer Rabbit had to do some fast talking. "You can cook me up in a big ol' pot, but please don't throw me into dat briar patch yonder!" cried Brer Rabbit.

Brer Fox thought for a moment. "Now, maybe dat stew would be too much bother for me. I'm a-gonna roast you up instead!"

"You can roast me an' serve me up with fried taters, but pleeease don't throw me in dat briar patch!" pleaded Brer Rabbit.

All this cooking was starting to sound like a lot of work to Brer Fox. Suddenly, Brer Fox knew just the thing to do.

"Seems to me jus' about the worst thing I kin do is throw you into dat ol' briar patch, Rabbit," said Brer Fox. "An' dat's jus' what I'm a-gonna do!"

And with that, Brer Fox swung Brer Rabbit over his head and threw him into the middle of the briar patch.

"Yow! Oh, I'm a-gonna die!" yowled Brer Rabbit as he sailed through the air.

But soon Brer Fox could hear Brer Rabbit hee-hawing and guffawing in gigglement. Brer Fox knew he'd been had again.

"Oh, Mister Fox, you shoulda known better! I was born in dis here briar patch! I'm as happy as a crawfish in a river bed!"

Brer Fox was hoppin' mad. "I got to git dat rabbit good, once an' for all. He's a-goin' to Miss Goose's birthday party tomorrow, so I'm a-gonna make real friendly-like, an' go an' walk over to dat party with him. An' when we git to crossin' the river, I'm a-gonna throw dat rabbit in!"

The next day, Brer Rabbit was at his house getting all spruced up for the party. When he saw Brer Fox come a-trottin' up his path, he wrapped himself up in a blanket and acted real sick-like.

"Oh, I'm sick as an ol' dawg, Mister Fox," sighed Brer Rabbit. "I ain't a-gonna make it to Miss Goose's party after all."

"This is a-gonna be jus' fine," thought Brer Fox. He said, "You gonna be sorry if you miss dat party, so I'm a-gonna carry you."

"You're mighty kind, Mister Fox. But surely I couldn't ride on your back without a saddle," said Brer Rabbit sneakily. While Brer Fox was gone, Brer Rabbit picked some flowers for Miss Goose and hid them.

Brer Fox came back wearing a saddle.

"You're mighty kind, Mister Fox, but surely I couldn't ride in dis saddle without a bridle to steer you along," said Brer Rabbit.

While Brer Fox went to fetch a bridle, Brer Rabbit found a brown paper bag. "I'm a-gonna give that fox a surprise he'll never forgit. He thinks he can outfox me, but I'm the foxiest rabbit this side of the Mississippi," Brer Rabbit said with chuckleness.

When Brer Fox returned, he was wearing a bridle as well as the saddle. "Rabbit," he said, "Miss Goose ain't a-gonna take it kindly if we're late for her party. You climb on up here now, an' let's git a-goin'." He chuckled to himself, thinking that soon he would be rid of that rabbit forever.

"You're terrible kind to an ol' sick rabbit like me, Mister Fox," said Brer Rabbit.

Soon they came to the river. As Brer Fox reached the middle of the bridge he thought, "Yep, this is just the spot."

But Brer Rabbit was ready for Brer Fox's sneaky trick. As soon as he felt Brer Fox stop, he filled the paper bag with air. He said, "What you stoppin' for, Mister Fox?"

"I'm a-gonna throw you into kingdom come, Rabbit!"

"Oh, no you're not!" shouted Brer Rabbit, popping that bag right over Brer Fox's ears.

"Yeeoow!" shrieked Brer Fox. He thought a hunter had taken a shot at him. He jumped up in the air like a mad grasshopper and took off down the other side of the bridge.

"Giddyup, you ol' nag!" cried Brer Rabbit. Poor Brer Fox just kept on galloping along, and right up to Miss Goose's house. When Brer Fox came galloping up with Brer Rabbit on his back, Miss Goose, Miss Sheep, and Miss Pig thought they had never seen anything so funny.

"Whoa!" shouted Brer Rabbit. Brer Fox skidded to a stop right on the doorstep. "Aft'noon, ladies," said Brer Rabbit. "I am very sorry for bein' late, but my ol' horse here jus' don't run like he used to."

Miss Goose, Miss Sheep, and Miss Pig burst with gigglement. They thought Brer Rabbit sure got Brer Fox good this time.

Poor old Brer Fox sat in the front yard of Miss Goose's house, sputtering and gluttering. "That rabbit tricked me good dis time," he fumed. "I don' know how I'm a-gonna do it, but I'm a-gonna git dat rabbit one day, once an' for all."

Ever since that day, ol' Brer Fox has kept trying to outsmart Brer Rabbit. And ever since that day, sneaky Brer Rabbit has been just one step ahead of Brer Fox.

So if you ever see a rabbit hopping around in a briar patch, or if you glimpse a fox snooping around a farmer's garden, it just might be crafty ol' Brer Rabbit and sneaky ol' Brer Fox trying to outfox each other again.

Brer Rabbit was smaller than Brer Fox, but he used his wits to beat Brer Fox again and again. Brer Rabbit was clever enough to know that he could not win in a match of strength. Instead, he came up with ideas to outsmart Brer Fox, and made Brer Fox do the exact opposite of what he had been planning to do.

Being clever is the best weapon against a bully. If someone bigger than you tries to scare you, use your wits to defend yourself or to avoid a confrontation altogether. It will show who the bigger person really is.

Androcles and the Lion

A Tale of Friendship

Androcles and the Lion

Adapted by Sarah Toast
Illustrated by Yuri Salzman

In ancient Rome there lived a poor slave named Androcles. His cruel master made him work from daybreak until long past nightfall. One day, he decided to run away, even though it was against the law.

Clouds covered the moon that night, and Androcles crossed the open fields unseen.

Eventually, Androcles found a sheltered place at the foot of a tall tree. There he lay himself down and fell fast asleep.

When Androcles awoke, he hiked deeper into the woods so he wouldn't be found. Day after day, Androcles searched for food, but found none. Androcles grew so weary and weak that at last he was afraid he wouldn't live through the night. He had just enough strength to creep up to the mouth of a cave he had passed many times. Androcles crawled in and fell into a deep sleep.

As Androcles lay sleeping, a lion was hunting in the woods nearby. The lion caught a small animal for his supper. He ate his meal beside a stream in the woods. Then he set off for his cave as the morning began to fill the sky with light.

In front of the cave where Androcles slept, the lion stepped on a large thorn and let out an angry roar, which woke Androcles with a terrible start. From the mouth of the cave, Androcles could see the lion rolling on the ground in pain. The lion's roars echoed loudly in the cave.

Androcles was terrified that the lion would attack him. But the lion held out his hurt paw to Androcles. Even from a distance, Androcles could see the thorn.

Androcles gathered courage and slowly sat down near the beast. To Androcles's astonishment, the huge lion flopped his great paw into the young man's lap.

Androcles spoke soothing words as he carefully pulled the thorn from the lion's paw. The lion seemed to understand that Androcles was helping him. When the thorn was out, the lion rubbed his head against Androcles and purred a rumbling purr.

Androcles was no longer afraid. The lion was very grateful to Androcles, and didn't even mind that Androcles had moved into his cave. They became fast friends.

The lion slept most of the day. And at night, he hunted for food while Androcles slept. In the morning, the lion would bring fresh meat to Androcles, who would build a little fire to cook his newly caught meal.

Every morning after Androcles ate, he and the lion played in the woods nearby. Androcles would scratch the lion behind the ears and pet his sleek back.

One morning, as Androcles was cooking what the lion had brought him, four soldiers suddenly appeared and surprised him.

"We saw the smoke from your fire," they said. "We have come to arrest you for running away from your master."

Androcles did not know what to do. He tried to run from the soldiers, but they were too fast for him. They caught him and tied his hands behind his back. Androcles cried out as the soldiers tried to carry him off.

The lion awoke with a start. Before he could help Androcles, two soldiers threw a strong rope net over him. They attached the ends of the net to two stout poles and carried the angry lion out of the woods.

Androcles was taken to a huge arena in Rome, where people were entertained watching battles fought on the sandy floor.

One soldier said to Androcles, "Your punishment is to fight a hungry lion!"

The soldiers took Androcles to a prison under the arena seats and left him alone in his cell. Androcles had never felt so scared or so alone. It was a long time before the soldiers came back for him.

Suddenly, Androcles heard a trumpet blast. Then the bars to his prison cell were opened. A soldier took Androcles and pushed him onto the field.

Androcles found himself alone in the middle of the huge arena. He noticed a large cage at the end of the field. When a lion's roar sounded throughout the arena, the people cheered with excitement.

The trumpet sounded a second time. In a moment, a lean lion bounded out of the cage, roaring with hunger. The people sitting in the arena shouted, "Hooray!"

The lion paused briefly, and in that moment, Androcles recognized his friend.

The lion let out another thundery roar and bounded across the arena in three long leaps. He stopped right in front of Androcles and gently lifted his big paw.

Androcles gave a mighty shout of joy. "Lion, you remember me!" he cried. He took the lion's paw in his hand and patted it lovingly. Androcles scratched the lion behind the ears, just as he had done before.

The crowd was stunned into silence. No one had never seen anything like this in the arena. Everyone turned to each other and started talking at once. They wanted to know what this boy's secret was for taming the ferocious lion.

The emperor, who watched every battle in the arena, motioned for silence. Then he called Androcles to approach him.

"How did you tame this vicious lion?" the emperor asked Androcles.

"I merely helped him when he needed help, Your Majesty," Androcles replied.

The emperor could see that Androcles and the lion were true friends. The emperor freed Androcles and the lion. The lion returned to the cave in the wild woods, and Androcles became a free man in Rome.

Androcles often went for walks in the woods to visit his good friend, who always greeted him as if they had never been apart.

· Friendship ·

Androcles and the lion made an unlikely pair, but their friendship proved to be strong and true. When Androcles removed the thorn from the lion's paw, a friendship based on trust and compassion was born. It was this bond that kept the lion from attacking Androcles in the arena.

Friendships are best when they are based on trust. Friends need to be able to count on each other to be caring and thoughtful to one another. Do you have a best friend? What do you like about your friend? What do you think he or she likes best about you?

The Brownie of Blednock

A Tale of Generosity

The Brownie of Blednock

Adapted by Jennifer Boudart
Illustrated by Gwen Connelly

Nighttime was falling over the town of Blednock, and the people who lived there were doing what they did every evening. No one knew it, but something special was about to happen. It all began with a humming noise. The townspeople lined up along Main Street and looked down the road.

They could see somebody coming. People began to whisper to each other. Who was this visitor to Blednock? Why was he humming?

No one had seen a person who looked like this before. The stranger was as small as a boy, but he had a long, brown beard. He wore a long, pointed hat and tiny, curled-up shoes. He walked closer and closer, and the humming got louder and louder.

That's when they heard what the stranger was humming: "Any work for Aiken-Drum? Any work for Aiken-Drum?"

What was Aiken-Drum? No one seemed to know. The people were more curious than ever. Then Granny, the wisest woman in the town, had something to say. "I think Aiken-Drum is what our visitor calls himself," she announced. "I believe he is a brownie."

Granny shook the brownie's hand, and said, "Speak up, Brownie." So he did.

"The ways of brownies are different from the ways of people," he said. "In our land, we learn to do good by serving others."

The little brownie explained that he was from somewhere far away, and there was not enough work in his land. "I just need a dry place to sleep and something warm to drink at bedtime," said the brownie. In return, he promised to do any kind of work.

"If there's a town that needs a helping hand, it's Blednock," said Granny. She was right. The new church needed building. The old bridge needed mending.

And that is how a brownie came to live in the town of Blednock. All of the townspeople chipped in to try to make the visitor comfortable in his new home.

The blacksmith let Aiken-Drum sleep in a dry corner of his barn. He gave the brownie just a simple horse's blanket to keep warm at night, for that is what Aiken-Drum had requested.

"We brownies don't need anything fancy. A simple blanket from the stable will do," reminded Aiken-Drum.

The blacksmith knew that keeping his sleeping area simple was a way to show respect for Aiken-Drum's wishes.

Every morning, the blacksmith found only an empty mug in the barn and the horse blanket folded neatly in the corner.

Each evening, Granny brought Aiken-Drum plain tea. The rest of the townspeople tried in vain to spot him at work. It always seemed that he was hurrying off to one place or another.

Soon, all of the people of Blednock were sharing stories about his magical work.

"Aiken-Drum fixed a broken wheel on my wagon last night. He must have known I was going to take my grain to the miller today," chuckled Baker Smith. "I am forever grateful to that curious little brownie."

"While I was asleep with fever, Aiken-Drum came," said Mother Jones. "He cleaned my whole house and cooked a big batch of soup!" she said.

"Aiken-Drum brought all my sheep to safety. He took them into the barn just before last night's storm!" said Farmer Adams. "And he did it so quietly, too. I didn't hear a thing until the storm kicked in."

More and more stories were being told of the good work that Aiken-Drum was doing. Wherever work needed to be done, he was there. The town was looking better than it ever had. The new church was even prettier than anyone had hoped.

Aiken-Drum did take breaks from time to time. On still evenings, the brownie sat by the river. He was never alone long. The children of Blednock would come join him.

Children loved Aiken-Drum. He loved them, too. They crowded around, giggling and asking to play this game or that:

"Tell us a story, Aiken-Drum."

"Play hide-and-seek, Aiken-Drum."

Aiken-Drum would start a bonfire and tell stories and play with the children until their parents called them for dinner. When the children went off to their houses, the brownie went off to work. That's the way Aiken-Drum liked it.

Almost everyone thought things around Blednock were better than ever. Only Miss Daisy thought differently. "It's not right for a brownie to work so hard for so little," she said.

Miss Daisy's neighbors shook their heads at her. "Aiken-Drum made it plain," they would say with a sigh. "Brownies work only for the love of making people happy."

Miss Daisy just sniffed. She was sure he needed something more. He simply was too shy to ask. Why, who wouldn't want more than a stable and a horse blanket?

Finally, Miss Daisy decided to do what she thought was best. Everyone would thank her for it later, Aiken-Drum most of all.

One night, Miss Daisy tiptoed into the blacksmith's barn. The brownie wasn't there. Miss Daisy placed a pair of her husband's pants next to his mug.

Well, you can guess what happened. Aiken-Drum took one look at those pants and knew what was happening. Someone had tried to pay him! His new friends had forgotten what mattered most to a brownie, so he disappeared that very night.

The people were heartbroken, and the children saddest of all. But sometimes, when the wind was just right, they could hear faint humming across the river, and they knew their brownie was off helping another town.

• Generosity •

When someone does a good deed from the goodness of his or her own heart, it is called generosity. A generous person does not expect a reward or recognition. The brownie, Aiken-Drum, was generous with the work he did for the people of Blednock. He did not want money or a reward for his work. He did not need praise or a fancy home. He worked simply for the sake of helping people who needed a hand.

Whom would you consider a generous person? How has this person shown his or her generosity? In what ways can you show that you are generous?

Icaurus and Daedalus

A Tale of Obedience

Icaurus and Daedalus

Adapted by Sarah Toast
Illustrated by John Hanley

Long ago in ancient Greece there lived a clever man named Daedalus. He was a great inventor, and a skillful engineer and architect. He was born and lived in Athens.

One day King Minos of Crete called Daedalus to build a labyrinth, or maze, to imprison the Minotaur, a monster that was half man and half bull. The labyrinth had so many false turns and dead ends that no one who entered it could ever find a way out.

When the labyrinth was finished, the angry Minotaur was sealed inside it. King Minos was satisfied that the monster was safely locked away.

Daedalus had been on Crete for a long time. He wanted to return home. He went to King Minos and said, "With your permission, I shall take my leave. My work is done, and I wish to return to Athens with my son."

"You will do no such thing," said King Minos. "You know the labyrinth's secret. How do I know you won't tell somebody how to navigate the twisting passageways?"

"I pledge that I will do no such thing," protested Daedalus.

But the king ordered his guards to lock Daedalus and his son, Icarus, in a tall tower.

Despite all of the good Daedalus had done for the king, Daedalus and Icarus were kept under close guard in the prison tower.

"Father, are we going to be locked up here forever?" asked Icarus.

"I am a great inventor, Icarus," replied Daedalus. "This is a difficult problem, but I shall think of a solution."

After days of being locked in their prison, Daedalus and Icarus needed fresh air. They climbed the stairway to the rooftop of the tower. Its great height made Daedalus fearful for Icarus's safety.

From the rooftop, Daedalus and Icarus watched the gulls and eagles soaring and gliding through the air. Daedalus studied with fascination the great wings as the birds flew close to the tower.

Daedalus watched closely the way the birds used their wings to take off and fly. He studied the way feathers fit together to cover the birds' wings. He noted the weight and the size of the wings in proportion to the birds' bodies.

"Icarus, my son, I have an idea to get us out of here," said Daedalus. "I want you to help me catch some birds. We need many feathers of all sizes."

Icarus watched his father intently as he laid out a row of long feathers. Then his father laid a row of smaller feathers below that. He sewed them together with thread and a needle that he carried in his pouch.

Daedalus laid down many more rows of feathers. Finally, he softened some beeswax and fastened the rows of feathers together.

At last Daedalus was finished. He held up a beautiful pair of wings! Daedalus tied the wings to his body with thin strips of leather. Cautiously, he fluttered the wings.

Daedalus moved his arms up and down with strong beats. As the wings moved, he could feel himself lifting from the floor.

Daedalus then made a smaller set of wings for his son, and instructed him to wait on the roof while he tested the wings.

Daedalus spread his wings and caught the wind. Out he soared, lifting on the air currents, like a bird. Then he returned to the tower and tied his son's wings to the boy.

Icarus couldn't wait any longer to try out his wings. He stood on tiptoe at the edge of the tower, flapped his wings, and took off. He swooped and soared, like his father. As he flew, he shouted for joy. "I'm a bird! I'm a god!" he cried.

"Icarus! Come back!" shouted Daedalus. "Come back to the tower!"

"Son, we have much to learn about flying," said Daedalus. "We will have to practice to become strong enough to fly all the way across the Aegean Sea," Daedalus explained.

Daedalus and Icarus practiced flying every day. Their muscles became strong. When Daedalus judged that he and Icarus were ready to make the long trip over the sea, he sat Icarus down.

"Son, if you fly too low, too close to the waves," Daedalus explained, "your feathers will get wet, and your wings will be too heavy. And if you fly too high, the sun will melt the wax that holds your wings together."

"I understand, Father," said Icarus, but he was barely listening.

The boy ran to the very edge of the rooftop and leaped off. He flapped his wings and headed for the sea, with Daedalus close behind him.

When the two reached the blue Aegean, Daedalus shouted a reminder to his son. The father and son rode the rising air currents. They made long, slow turns, first one way and then the other in the brilliant blue sky. After a while, Daedalus took the lead.

Icarus did a somersault, then caught up with this father. Daedalus gestured for Icarus to stay at a safe middle level.

But Icarus wanted to fly up to where the gods lived. While Daedalus flew on in front, Icarus rose up and up. The sun felt good on his back, and Icarus rose even higher.

The same warm sun soon melted the wax on Icarus's wings. First only a few feathers, and then many, slipped off as the wax turned to liquid. Suddenly, Icarus dropped straight down, into the cold sea.

When Daedalus looked back, he could no longer see his son. At last, Daedalus saw the feathers floating on the sea.

Daedalus wept as he flew on alone. If his beloved son had listened, they would be flying to freedom together.

• Obedience •

Icarus got carried away and did not obey his father's warning about flying too close to the sun. He wanted only to play with his new wings, and did not listen to the advice that Daedalus—a scientist, who understood what the sun's heat could do—gave him.

Children often think that they don't need the advice that adults give them. They don't always remember that adults were once children, too. They have made mistakes and learned from their experiences. Adults tell you what to do because they care, and don't want you to get hurt doing things they know can be dangerous.

The Wild Swans

A Tale of Perseverance

The Wild Swans

Adapted by Brian Conway
Illustrated by Kathy Mitchell

Once there was a king who had much happiness and great fortune. Of all his treasures, he was proudest of his four children. His three sons were fine and strong, and his daughter, Elise, seemed the dearest, sweetest, and kindest child in all the world.

Then one day the king hurried to find Elise. "You are in danger," he told her, for he had wicked enemies who believed no one should have the happiness the king had.

"I fear for your safety," the king told his daughter. "During the night, your brothers were taken away from us. I know not where. I cannot stand to lose you, too."

The king told the princess to go with his trusted servants, who would take her to safety in their home in the forest.

"When you're old enough," said the king, "find your brothers and come back to me."

He kissed her good-bye. Elise did as her father said. She lived hidden away in the servants' house for many years. She was treated well, but she was very unhappy. Elise longed to see her three beloved brothers and her father again.

When Elise was old enough, she set off to find her brothers. She had no idea where to look, but she had a feeling inside that told her they needed her help.

After several days of wandering, Elise met an old woman at the seashore.

"I am looking for my three brothers," Elise told her. "They are fine, strong princes. Have you seen them?"

"I have seen nothing all day but three white swans with golden crowns on their heads," the old woman said, showing Elise three white feathers. Elise clutched them close to her and fell asleep while she waited for the swans to return.

Just before sunset, Elise woke up to see three majestic swans gliding down to the shore. As the last ray of sunshine disappeared, the three swans changed into three princes—her brothers! They held her close and told her what had happened.

Many years ago, an evil sorcerer had come to the castle. This sorcerer vowed to ruin the king's happiness, and turned the three handsome princes into swans. Since that day, they had lived as swans during the day and humans during the night.

"We have seen our father," the eldest brother told Elise. "He serves the sorcerer against his will."

Elise promised to help free her brothers from the wicked spell. Her brothers told her of an enchanted land far across the sea where they might find a way to break the spell.

"Take me with you," Elise urged them. "I know I can help."

Her brothers crafted a net to carry Elise in. They rushed to reach land by nightfall, or else all three brothers and their sister would drop into the sea.

After two days' flight, they arrived where it was said that the fairy queen, Morgana, lived. Surely she would know how to help them. Elise's brothers found her a cave to rest in while they searched for Queen Morgana.

That night, Queen Morgana came to Elise in a dream.

"Only you can free your brothers," she told Elise. "But you must sacrifice greatly."

Elise listened carefully.

"Craft a shirt for each brother from rose petals," Queen Morgana said. "When you cover the swans with them, the spell will be broken. You may not speak until the shirts are made. If you utter even one word, your brothers will be swans forever."

With that, Queen Morgana disappeared. Elise awoke to find the cave surrounded with hundreds of lovely rosebushes. She knew what she had to do.

Elise set to work immediately. She used the roses' prickly thorns as needles to string the petals together. Elise worked tirelessly, day and night. Her brothers visited her, but Elise didn't dare speak.

Soon Elise had but one sleeve left to sew. But that day a woodcutter and his wife came upon Elise's garden. The woodcutter's wife loved roses, and had a lovely garden herself.

"What are you doing out in the woods alone?" she asked, but Elise didn't dare respond. "Poor child, come with us. We'll give you proper food and rest."

Elise did not want to leave the garden. She wanted to finish the third shirt.

Elise gathered up the shirts and as many roses as she could carry.

She stayed with the woodcutter and his wife for many days. At night, she stayed awake to finish the last shirt. But before long, Elise ran out of rose petals.

That night, she creeped out of the house and plucked petals from the garden.

At sunrise, the woodcutter's wife found her in the garden. "Ungrateful girl!" she shouted. "You've ruined my roses!"

At that moment Elise's brothers arrived to visit her. Elise quickly spread the three shirts over the swans.

Before her eyes, the swans became men!

Elise ran to her brothers' arms. Anxious to speak now that the spell had been broken, she explained everything to the woodcutter and his wife. "I'm sorry that I have been so difficult, when you have been so kind," said Elise. "We will repay you."

Elise and her brothers took all of the rosebushes from the forest cave and planted them in the woodcutter's garden.

Then they set off for the sorcerer's castle. The sorcerer was so angered by the spell's failure, he disappeared forever. The king was overjoyed to see his children, and the four set up a new home together in the castle. In the garden, they planted rosebushes.

• Perseverance •

Perseverance is when you strive for something and don't give up, even when it seems like the odds are against you. Elise worked day and night, without speaking, to break the spell cast on her brothers. No matter how hard her task seemed, Elise did not stop. Nothing was more important to Elise than saving her brothers.

When a task is important to you, it is worth all of your effort. Imagine if a member of your family were in trouble, and you were the only one who could help. Wouldn't you do everything you could to help, even if it were very difficult?

Ali Baba

A Tale of Loyalty

Ali Baba

Adapted by Brian Conway
Illustrated by Anthony Lewis

In a town in Persia there lived a poor woodcutter called Ali Baba. All he ever wanted was to own a shop, be generous with his neighbors, and have plenty for his family.

One day Ali Baba was cutting wood in the forest. He saw a troop of men on horseback approaching. Ali Baba feared they were robbers, so he climbed a tree to hide.

Ali Baba counted 40 men. Their leader dismounted and stood next to a bush in front of a rock wall. He shouted, "Open, sesame!"

A secret door opened, revealing a cave.

The leader and the other robbers entered the cave. As they prepared to leave, the leader closed the door, saying, "Shut, sesame!" Then the thieves rode away.

When he was sure they were gone, Ali Baba stepped close and shouted, "Open, sesame!" And the door opened.

Ali Baba stepped through the threshold to find a large room filled with all sorts of valuables, made from gold, silver, and jewels. He feared the robbers might soon return and quickly gathered as much gold as he could carry. Now he could finally open his shop!

Ali Baba remembered in his haste to say, "Shut, sesame!" when he left the cave.

Ali Baba did not notice that he dropped a single gold coin at the base of the bush that covered the secret door.

A few weeks later, the leader caught sight of the coin glimmering in the sunlight. "How could you risk revealing our hiding place?" he asked angrily.

But none of the thieves remembered dropping the coin.

"Then we have been found out," the leader growled. He paced for several minutes with the thieves waiting anxiously for him to speak. Then he announced, "We must learn who is newly rich in the town. That man and all his family must pay."

By now Ali Baba had in fact opened his shop. He was a fair and generous shop owner. He and his family were happy.

Ali Baba hired a helper named Morgiana. She was a very clever and beautiful young lady, and cared for Ali Baba and his family.

One day, a stranger came calling at the shop. He asked Morgiana many questions about the owner. The stranger's questions worried Morgiana.

The disguised thief returned to the cave and said, "The man who found us out is called Ali Baba. He lives behind his new shop in town. He was a poor woodcutter only a few weeks ago."

"Go back there at nightfall," the leader ordered. "Mark his house with this white chalk, and later, we will all go to the marked house and finish him."

One of the robbers moved through the shadows, using his chalk to mark Ali Baba's home. Little did he know that clever Morgiana had spotted him. After the thief marked Ali Baba's door, she followed with her own white chalk and marked the rest of the doors in town.

When the leader and his thieves arrived later that night, they found every door was marked. They did not know which house to attack, so they crept away in shame.

The leader decided to use all his power against Ali Baba. The 40 thieves gathered together and made a plan. The leader would disguise himself as an oil merchant. He would lead a train of mules that carried 39 barrels. The thieves would hide inside the barrels and await the signal. Early that night, the thieves arrived at Ali Baba's shop.

"I have brought some oil to sell at market tomorrow," the leader lied. "But tonight I need a place to stay. Will you take me in?"

Ali Baba was as generous as usual. "Of course you may stay here," he replied. "Leave your cargo in back. There is hay there for the mules. Then come in for dinner."

In the yard, the leader whispered to his men, "Wait until you hear my signal. Then, leave your barrels and storm the house."

Later that night, Morgiana was cleaning up when her lamp ran out of oil. Then she remembered the oil barrels out back.

She walked up to a barrel. A voice whispered, "Is it time?"

Morgiana sensed danger. She answered, "Not yet, but soon." Then, gathering some hay around each barrel, Morgiana lit the hay with a torch. The 39 cowardly thieves coughed from the smoke. They popped out from their barrels and ran away to keep from getting burned.

When the leader made his signal, none of his men moved. The next day, he returned to the cave to find his 39 robbers gone. Now on his own, the thief decided he would have to use all his cunning to plan his revenge.

The leader opened a shop across the road from Ali Baba's shop and lived as Cogia Hassan for many months. He waited in this disguise until just the right moment.

After a while, Ali Baba invited the new shop owner over for dinner. Cogia Hassan graciously accepted and brought a basket of fine goods.

But Cogia Hassan carried a dagger in his cloak, intended for Ali Baba and his son.

Morgiana saw the dagger and quickly came up with a plan. She wore long, flowing scarves, then entered the dining room to dance for the guest.

Morgiana danced close to Cogia Hassan. Stepping behind him, Morgiana wrapped the scarf around his arms. He could not move.

"What are you doing?" Ali Baba cried.

"He is your enemy," she explained. "He has a dagger!" Ali Baba's son seized the dagger, and the thief was sent to prison.

"We owe you our lives," Ali Baba said. "Please marry my son and join our family."

Morgiana agreed, and they celebrated with a splendid wedding.

• Loyalty •

Morgiana, who worked for Ali Baba, was very loyal. She helped Ali Baba and his family again and again, although she was not a member of their family. She knew that she couldn't let something bad happen to people who always treated her with kindness.

Loyalty is being there for someone and helping him or her through tough times. It is showing that person you will stand by him or her when others have turned their backs. Have you ever heard someone be described as loyal? What do you think made that peron so loyal?

The Nightingale

A Tale of Friendship

The Nightingale

Adapted by Lisa Harkrader
Illustrated by Robin Moro

Many years ago, the emperor of China lived in a palace surrounded by beautiful gardens that visitors from all over the world came to admire.

One day, a fisherman led some of these visitors into the forest to see a nightingale that lived there. They grumbled, "We came all the way out here to see a plain gray bird?"

But then the nightingale opened its mouth. Its voice was pure and strong. Its song was lovelier than anything the visitors had ever heard.

The nightingale became known as the most beautiful thing in China. Everyone had heard of this remarkable bird. Everyone, that is, except the emperor and all who lived in the palace. Even the Japanese emperor wanted to see the nightingale.

The emperor summoned his prime minister. "The emperor of Japan arrives in two days," the emperor said. "He expects to see this nightingale. Search until you find it."

The prime minister searched everywhere. But he could not find the nightingale.

The emperor was worried. He now summoned all the palace guards to help the prime minister find the bird.

The next morning, and the one after that, the prime minister and the guards searched again, but still could not find the nightingale.

"The emperor of Japan will be here today," he told them. "You must find me this magnificent nightingale."

The prime minister trekked deep into the woods. He was about to give up when he came upon the fisherman, who led him to the nightingale.

The prime minister marched back into the palace as the Japanese emperor arrived.

"So this is the most beautiful thing in all of China," said the emperor of Japan. "I must say, he looks rather plain."

Suddenly, the nightingale opened his mouth. Out came the most beautiful song anyone had ever heard. The emperor of Japan was speechless. The emperor of China cried tears of joy.

Day after day the nightingale's song filled the palace. People crowded in to hear the beautiful music. Someone always said, "Too bad he doesn't look as lovely as he sounds."

These comments made the emperor very angry. The nightingale's song had brought him such joy. So the emperor gave the nightingale a golden perch, adorned with ribbons and bells, to sit on. Now he looked almost as lovely as his voice sounded.

One day a gift arrived from the emperor of Japan. "This is a small token compared with the joy your bird gave me," he wrote.

The Chinese emperor opened the box to find a replica of the nightingale, encrusted with emeralds, sapphires, and rubies. On its back was a silver key. When the emperor wound the key, the mechanical bird sang one of the nightingale's songs, though it did not sound as sweet as the real nightingale. Still, the emperor was pleased.

"Now you can rest," he told the real nightingale.

"Finally!" said the people. "A nightingale that looks as lovely as it sounds."

The people asked to hear the new bird over and over. They ignored the real nightingale, so he flew home to the forest.

Only one person noticed that the bird had gone—the emperor. "Maybe it's for the best," the emperor sighed. "He will be happier in the forest."

The people never grew tired of the mechanical bird's song. It played over and over, day after day, until one morning, with a loud twang and a pop, the bird stopped.

The emperor called in the watchmaker.

"A spring has sprung," the watchmaker proclaimed. "I'll fix it, but you'll have to be careful. Only wind it on special occasions."

The emperor missed the real nightingale. He grew sick and weak, and nothing helped. The old fisherman heard of the emperor's illness and told the nightingale.

The nightingale flew straight to the emperor's chambers. He perched on his bed and began to sing his beautiful song.

The emperor opened his eyes. "You came back," he whispered. Tears of joy streamed down his face. The emperor sat up in bed and the color returned to his cheeks. The two old friends visited late into the night.

The emperor grew strong again, and was soon able to walk the palace gardens once more, with the nightingale always by his side.

The emperor of China found more than just a beautiful voice in the nightingale. He also found a good friend. Nothing could take the bird's place, and the emperor was sad and lonely without him. The nightingale was a true companion to the emperor. He sat by his bed and sang to the emperor when the emperor needed him most.

Sometimes we make friends in the most unlikely places. The emperor didn't realize how good a friend the nightingale was until he was gone. Whom do you consider your friend? What would you miss about your friend if he or she went away?